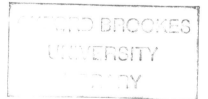

For Matthew and Andrew

First published in Great Britain 1997
1 3 5 7 9 10 8 6 4 2

Copyright © 1997 by Benedict Blathwayt
Benedict Blathwayt has asserted his right
under the Copyright, Designs and Patents Act, 1988
to be identified as the author of this work

First published in Great Britain 1997
by Julia MacRae
an imprint of Random House
20 Vauxhall Bridge Road, London SW1V 2SA

Random House Australia (Pty) Ltd
20, Alfred Street, Milsons Point, Sydney, NSW 2061, Australia

Random House New Zealand Ltd
18 Poland Road, Glenfield, Auckland 10, New Zealand

Random House South Africa (Pty) Ltd
Endulini, 5A Jubilee Road, Parktown 2193, South Africa

A CIP catalogue record for this book is
available from the British Library

ISBN 1 85681 573 0

Printed in Singapore

LITTLE RED TRAIN
TO THE RESCUE

Benedict Blathwayt

Julia MacRae Books

LONDON SYDNEY AUCKLAND JOHANNESBURG

One wet and windy day, Duffy
Driver lit the fire in the little red
train and collected three trucks
from the goods yard.

The trucks were soon loaded and Duffy Driver and the little
red train set off for Birchcombe village, high up in the hills.
Chuff-chuff, chuffitty-chuff...

But as they came round a bend, what did they see...

Animals on the line!
Duffy put on the brakes with a scree...eee...ch
and the little red train stopped just in time.

When the animals were back in the
farmyard, the little red train set off again.
Chuff-chuff, chuffitty-chuff...

But as they came round a bend, what did they see...

The river had flooded the road!
Duffy put on the brakes with a scree...eee...ch
and the little red train stopped just in time.

They rescued the passengers from the bus on
the bridge and the little red train set off again.
Chuff-chuff, chuffitty-chuff...
But as they came round a bend, what did they see...

The wind had blown down a tree!
Duffy put on the brakes with a scree...eee...ch
and the little red train stopped just in time.

Everyone helped to move the tree
and the little red train set off again.
Chuff–chuff, chuffitty–chuff...

But the track got steeper and steeper and
the little red train hotter and hotter until...

P O P! HISSSSS! The safety valve blew off the boiler!
Duffy Driver put on the brakes with a scree...eee...ch
and stopped to let the little red train cool down.

Up in the hills there was snow,
so they set off again more slowly.
Chuff-chuff-chuff, chuu...ff, chuff...itty-chu...ff...
But as they came round a bend, what did they see...

A great pile of snow was blocking the line!
Duffy put on the brakes with a scree...eee...ch
and the little red train stopped just in time.

They all helped to clear the snow
and the little red train set off again.
Chuff-chuff, chuffitty-chuff...

But as they came to the last stretch
of line what did they find...

The points had frozen!
The little red train went off the wrong way.
Duffy put on the brakes with a scree...eee...ch
and the little red train stopped just in time.

The signalman poured hot water on
the points and with a chuff-chuff,
chuffitty-chuff the little red train ran
on towards the station at Birchcombe...

POST OFFICE

Everyone was there to greet them.
Duffy Driver blew the whistle, whee...eee...eee
and put on the brakes with a scree...eee...ch and the
little red train stopped at the platform just in time.

The passengers climbed down and helped to unload the supplies...

and Duffy Driver was given a special tea by the postmistress.

Then Duffy got back into the driver's
cab and after he had blown the whistle,
whee...eee...eee, the little red train raced
back home. It was downhill all the way.

OFFICE

Chuffitty-chuffitty,
chuffitty-chuff...